W9-CZN-297

RIDER WOOFSON

THE VERY FIRST CASE

BY WALKER STYLES ● ILLUSTRATED BY BEN WHITEHOUSE

LITTLE SIMON

New York   London   Toronto   Sydney   New Delhi

This book is a work of fiction. Any references to historical events, real people, or real places are used fictitiously. Other names, characters, places, and events are products of the author's imagination, and any resemblance to actual events or places or persons, living or dead, is entirely coincidental.

LITTLE SIMON

An imprint of Simon & Schuster Children's Publishing Division
1230 Avenue of the Americas, New York, New York 10020
First Little Simon hardcover edition March 2018
Copyright © 2018 by Simon & Schuster, Inc.
Also available in a Little Simon paperback edition. All rights reserved, including the right of reproduction in whole or in part in any form. LITTLE SIMON is a registered trademark of Simon & Schuster, Inc., and associated colophon is a trademark of Simon & Schuster, Inc.
For information about special discounts for bulk purchases, please contact Simon & Schuster Special Sales at 1-866-506-1949 or business@simonandschuster.com.
The Simon & Schuster Speakers Bureau can bring authors to your live event. For more information or to book an event contact the Simon & Schuster Speakers Bureau at 1-866-248-3049 or visit our website at www.simonspeakers.com.
Designed by Laura Roode. The text of this book was set in ITC American Typewriter.
Manufactured in the United States of America 0218 FFG
2 4 6 8 10 9 7 5 3 1
Library of Congress Cataloging-in-Publication Data
Names: Styles, Walker, author. | Whitehouse, Ben, illustrator.
Title: The very first case / by Walker Styles ; illustrated by Ben Whitehouse.
Description: First Little Simon paperback edition. | New York : Little Simon, 2018. | Series: Rider Woofson ; 10 | Summary: "When Rider is interviewed by the *Pawston Paw Print*, he shares the untold story of how the P.I. Pack first met. As he relives their very first case, Rider discovers that someone has stolen all the past evidence!"—Provided by publisher. | Identifiers: LCCN 2017038348 | ISBN 9781534412712 (paperback) | ISBN 9781534412729 (hc) | ISBN 9781534412736 (eBook) | Subjects: | CYAC: Mystery and detective stories. | Detectives—Fiction. | Dogs—Fiction. | Animals—Fiction. | Stealing—Fiction. | BISAC: JUVENILE FICTION / Action & Adventure / General. | JUVENILE FICTION / Animals / General. | JUVENILE FICTION / Readers / Chapter Books. Classification: LCC PZ7.1.S82 Ver 2018 | DDC [Fic]—dc23
LC record available at https://lccn.loc.gov/2017038348

CONTENTS

chapter
ONE

News FLASH!

Flash! A large camera snapped a picture of the P.I. Pack office as if it were a true crime scene. The photographer was a kangaroo. He hopped around the office, taking more pictures. *Flash! Flash!*

"Hey! What's *hopping*—I mean, happening around here?" Westie Barker asked. The furry inventor pointed to a sign. "This area is top secret! Who are you?"

"It's okay, Westie," said lead detective Rider Woofson. "This is Scoops Hopper. He's a reporter from the *Pawston Paw Print*. He's writing a story on the P.I. Pack."

"Nice to meet you," Scoops said. He held up his camera and snapped another picture. *Flash!*

Westie rubbed his eyes. "I wish I could say the same."

"Don't mind Mr. Science," said a scruffy pup. "He's camera-shy."

It was Ziggy, the team's young-est detective. "Not me though! Snap away. What kind of story are you doing about Pawston's greatest detectives? Is it about the time we battled Icy Ivan, the evil Penguin Prowler? Good thing I brought my appetite. I saved the day by eating

my way out of an Ice Cream, You
Scream trap!"

Rider opened a cabinet drawer
and took out a case file. He showed
the reporter a picture of Icy Ivan
and Ziggy, after he ate all the ice
cream.

"Yes, well, you're not the only hero here," Westie added. "Don't forget about the case of the Mountain Goat Bandit. That sneaky thief could climb anything. In fact, he tried to rob the tallest building in Pawston. Too bad for him, I invented the Super Slip-Up. It's the world's most slippery stuff. The Mountain Goat Bandit slipped and slid all the way to prison."

Rider pulled out another case file to share with the reporter. Westie's hand-drawn map showed a path from the top of the building to the inside of a jail cell.

"This is great!" Scoops took another picture. "Wow, I am very impressed."

"You should be," Ziggy said. "I am very awesome."

"Ahem, I think the reporter was talking about me," Westie noted.

"Actually, I was talking about the files from your past cases," the kangaroo reporter said. "I've never seen such perfect organization."

Rider smiled. "A good detective must be organized. It's important to have access to every file at a moment's notice. You never know when something from the past will pop up again."

"So you have every file for every case you've ever worked?" Scoops asked. "Even your very *first* case?"

Rider walked over to another file cabinet and opened it. He pulled out a very old folder. "Take a seat, Scoops. You're going to love this story. It started way back, when we were in elementary school."

WELCOME TO PAWSTON ELEMENTARY

Rider Woofson stared out from his favorite spot. From here, he could see the crowd walk through the halls on their way to class. This was Pawston Elementary School. Every day, hundreds of students carried their backpacks, lunches, and notebooks, behaving as good students should.

But this school also had a darker side. That was where Rider came in. He wanted to be the greatest puppy detective in the school—maybe in the whole city.

Even before the morning bell, Rider already had a case.

The young detective spotted his first clue. It was a trail of pencil shavings. As he walked down the

hall, a teacher named Mr. Quick stopped him. "Rider, what are you doing? Your classroom is on the other side of the school."

"I'm on a case," Rider said. "There's been a report of missing pencils in math class. Mrs. Plus gave me a hall pass."

Rider showed Mr. Quick his hall pass. Then he continued on the trail. The pencil shavings led to a closed door. Rider was about to open it when another dog stepped out of the shadows.

"Don't bother. It's locked," she said. The dog had curly hair and held a magnifying glass.

"Who are you, and what are you doing here?" Rider asked.

The dog introduced herself. "I'm Rora Gooddog, and I'm working on a case. Some students are missing their erasers."

Rora pointed to the floor. "I followed a trail of pencil shavings to this door. Where there's a pencil, there's always an eraser."

"Wow, I'm looking for missing pencils!" Rider said. "Maybe we should work together?"

Rora nodded. "Let's go."

Rider and Rora put their ears to the locked door. There were strange clacking noises coming from the other side. Then there was a loud snap!

"How do we get in?" Rider asked.

Rora held up a giant set of keys. "The principal gave me these. All of the teachers are mad about grading tests that have wrong answers scratched out instead of erased."

She opened the door quietly. Inside, a group of bullies were taking turns trying to break pencils with other pencils. Tiny wooden shards were scattered all over the floor.

THWACK!

One bully snapped a pencil in half. "I win! Give me the eraser as a trophy."

"Looks like we found a secret pencil-fighting club!" whispered Rora. "What a terrible waste of school supplies."

She started to rush in, but Rider grabbed her arm. "Wait, we should report this to the principal's office. We solved the mystery—they can handle the bullies."

"Good idea," said Rora.

They ran to tell the principal, who broke up the pencil-fighting club immediately.

"Thanks, Rider and Rora," the principal said. "I have a feeling this isn't the last we'll hear from you two detectives."

SLIME TIME

A week later, Rider and Rora were outside eating lunch. They had been searching for a brand-new mystery to solve, but everything at Pawston Elementary was quiet . . . too quiet.

Suddenly, a group of students began screaming, "GROSS!" and ran away from the science room.

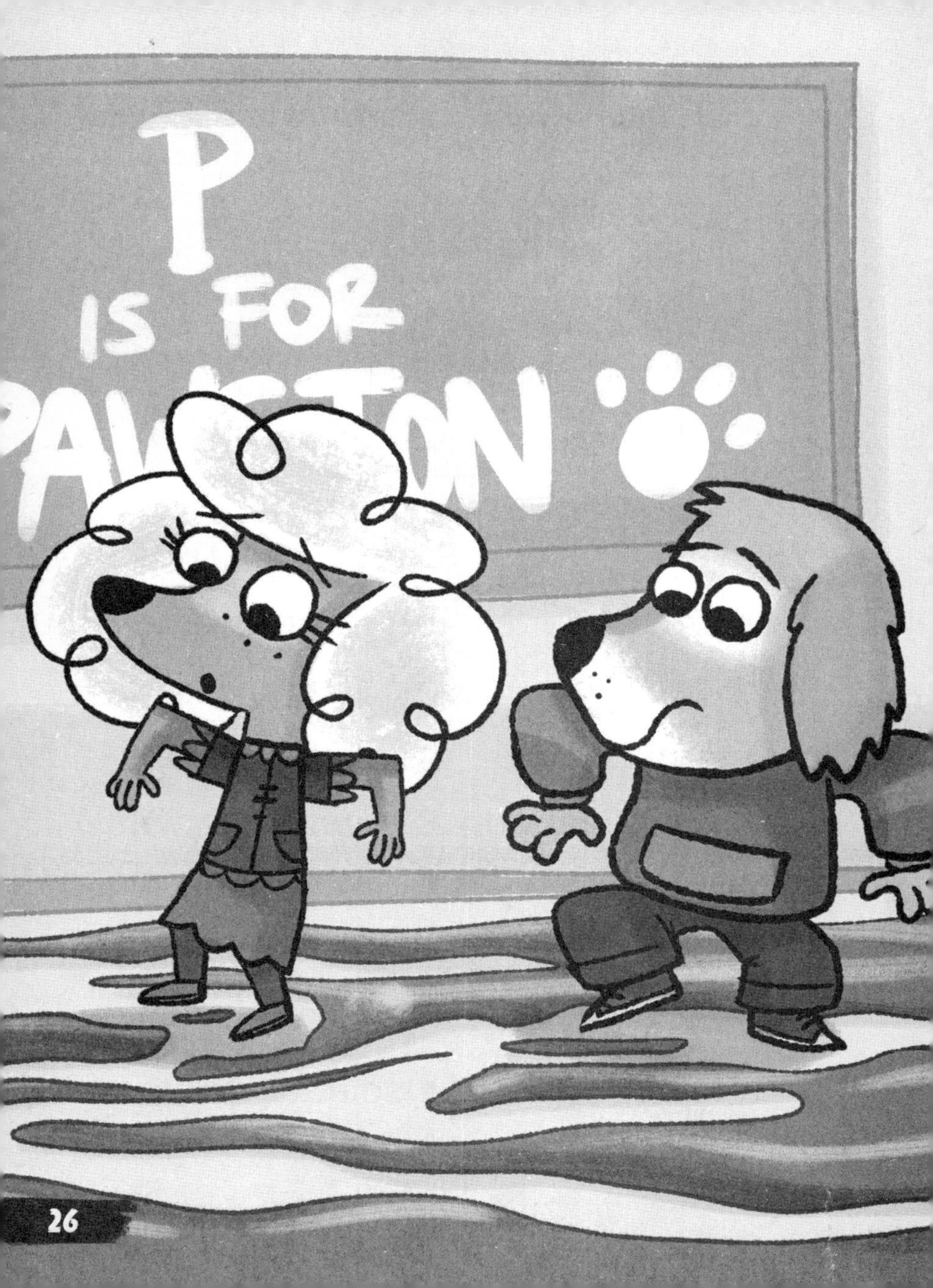
P
IS FOR

A wave of green slime oozed out of the windows.

Quickly, Rider and Rora made their way to the science room to find the source of the mess. They stepped carefully to avoid the green ooze in the halls.

A giant volcano stood in the middle of the classroom. It spewed wave after wave of the gross goo, like green lava that splatted everywhere. Next to the volcano was a small white dog wearing a lab coat and goggles. He was holding a giant magnet on a fishing rod.

Rider pointed. "Look! It's our first super-villain! Let's stop him!"

The detectives dove over the ooze toward the mad scientist.

"Freeze right there, Dr. Slime!" Rider shouted.

"Yeah, no more mess for you,
you messy dog," Rora added.

The pup waved back to them.
"Dr. Slime? No, I'm Westie Barker,
and I'm trying to stop this volcano
with my Super Soaker-Upper."

He held up the invention. "If I don't use it now, our whole school is going to get very icky and very sticky."

Rider looked unsure, but this Westie Barker might be their only hope. "Okay, but no funny business."

Westie nodded, and then he flipped a switch on the fishing rod. The magnet charged to life as he cast it into the sea of ooze. To Rider's surprise, the magnet began to soak up all the green slime.

"It worked!" Westie cheered.

"Yes, it did," Rora said. "Now, who would build a slime volcano in the first place?"

Westie hung his head sadly. "Maybe someone like me? You see, I'm an inventor, and I built this volcano. Then things got a little out of control."

"A little?" asked Rora. "More like *a lot* out of control."

Rider laughed. "Well, at least your Super Soaker-Upper worked."

Then the detective rubbed his

chin. "Hmm, would you like to join forces with us? I'm Rider, and this is Rora. We solve crimes and could use an inventor like you—even if things do get a little out of control sometimes."

Westie smiled. "Count me in."

MEATBALL MANIA

The school cafeteria was a great place to find mysteries. Rider, Rora, and Westie sat at their table trying to figure out what was in the Soup Surprise of the day.

Rider braved a whiff. "It smells like your volcano slime."

Westie tried to smell his soup but knocked over the bowl.

The Soup Surprise spilled onto the floor and all over a tiny lunch lady who was walking by their table.

"Careful," snapped the lunch lady. She was wearing an apron three sizes too big and a hairnet that covered her entire head.

"Sorry!" Westie apologized, but the tiny lady huffed and walked into the kitchen.

"That's one angry lunch lady," Rora said.

"Hmm, if that's a lunch lady, I'll eat my hat," said Rider.

"You're not wearing a hat," said Westie.

"Then I'll get one," Rider said with a wink. "All great detectives have a cool hat."

"You'll buy a hat just to eat it?" Rora asked.

Before Rider could answer, a scuffle broke out from the kitchen. A panda bear in an apron burst

through the cafeteria. He was holding a giant pot of pasta and meatballs. The tiny lunch lady from before was clinging to the panda's apron.

Then a *real* lunch lady shouted from the kitchen. "Nab those noodle-nabbers!"

"We will stop those spaghetti stealers!" Rider cried out as the detectives jumped into action. The giant panda hurled meat-balls at them, and one hit Rider in

the face. "This is gonna be a messy mystery."

Westie pressed his belt buckle. It transformed into a large robot paw that swatted the meatballs away. Unfortunately, the meatballs smacked into other students. *Splat! Splat! Splat!*

"Sorry!" Westie cringed.

"Focus on catching the bad guys, Westie," Rora said.

Finally, Rider snagged a noodle and made it into a lasso. He tossed it, but he only caught the tiny lunch

lady. The panda bear escaped with
the lunch special.

"Aha! Got you, thief!" exclaimed Rider. He pulled off the tiny lunch lady's hairnet and apron to reveal a scrappy little puppy dog.

"*Bow-wowza!*" the young puppy barked. "I'm not the thief."

Rider lifted up the hairnet. "Then why were you wearing a disguise?"

The puppy let out a groan. "That's because I'm undercover, and you have to wear a good disguise to catch bad guys in the act!"

Rider still didn't believe him. "I think we caught you red-handed."

"Oh, that's just pasta sauce." The puppy looked at his paw and licked  it. "Listen, I'm Ziggy Fluffenscruff, and I've been after the Lunchtime Bandit for weeks. He's gotten away again, thanks to you. What am I going to eat for lunch now that all those yummy meatballs are gone?"

"Do you like Soup Surprise?" asked Westie.

"Yuck!" Ziggy made a gross face. "Who are you anyway?"

Rora put her arm around Ziggy. "We're the ones who are going to help you catch the Lunchtime Bandit."

chapter FIVE

Tex-Mex Mess Up

The next morning before school, Ziggy told his new friends about the Lunchtime Bandit.

"He always strikes at lunch and steals the special of the day." Ziggy's stomach growled. This case was already making him hungry. "I've asked around, and he's not one of the cafeteria cooks."

"No, he's a cafeteria *crook*!" Rora said.

"Exactly! And I love food more than anything," Ziggy said as he licked his lips. "We need to stop him before he strikes again. Today's special is my favorite . . . bean burritos!"

"Time for a plan," Rider said.

"Ooh, I have an idea," Westie said. "Let's replace the good beans

with rotten beans. That way, if we don't catch him, we can follow the stinky smell to wherever he's hiding!"

The young pups did just that with the help of the cafeteria workers.

At noon, the Lunchtime Bandit
showed up and grabbed the pot
filled with bad beans. When he
made a run for it, Rider jumped
out to block the exit. "Not
so fast, Bandit. Drop
those beans, and put
your paws up!"

"Whatever you say," the huge panda said with an evil laugh. Then he threw the disgusting beans right out the window.

Mrs. Turtle decided to have class outside that day. Her favorite student was named Ronald Ruffhouse. He was a total teacher's pet. He always studied and was always very polite. Every time Mrs. Turtle asked a question, Ronald raised his hand.

"Now, Ronald," Mrs. Turtle said, "I'm sure you know the answer, but let some of the other students have a turn."

"Yes, Mrs. Turtle," Ronald said. He put his hand down politely.

It was a perfectly normal day for Ronald, until a shower of stinky beans plopped all over him.

Suddenly, a giant panda ran out of the cafeteria with four puppies chasing him. The panda pointed at Ronald, who was covered head to

to paw in beans, and said, "Ew. Those beans have gone bad. Rotten luck!"

Ronald looked like he was about to burst into tears, but all his classmates were laughing and chanting, "ROTTEN RUFFHOUSE! ROTTEN RUFFHOUSE!"

"Oh no!" cried Rora. "The Bandit tossed our trap on that poor pup!"

"Whoa! That stinks!" said Ziggy as he darted by the bean scene.

"Keep focused on the Bandit!" Rider huffed as he ran, but the pups could not keep up with the panda.

"He's too fast," puffed Rora as she and Westie slowed down. "Who knew pandas could run like that."

With the Lunchtime Bandit gone and their bean plan ruined, the pups huddled up. It was time for a better plan.

chapter
SIX

THINGS GO BANANAS!

The junior detectives returned to the scene of the crime. Rider used his magnifying glass to look for clues. "To solve this case, we have to think like a criminal."

"First, we need to figure out how he snuck in," Rora said.

Ziggy nodded. "The Bandit uses disguises. Yesterday he was

a lunch lady. Once he dressed as a milkman. Another time he pretended to be a baker. The other day he dressed as a giant elephant delivering tiny pickles. He could be anybody!"

"How do you know these things?" asked Westie.

"I keep my ear to the ground," Ziggy said with a wink.

"I bet he came in through the skylight!" Rora said, pointing upward. "Bad guys love skylights."

"It's locked," said Rider. "I checked it already to make sure."

"What if he used an army of micro-bots to sneak inside and steal the food," said Westie. "That's what I would do."

"Nice try, but we saw the Bandit steal the food himself. Not any robots, small or big," Rider noted.

"Drats," Westie said. "I was hoping someone would invent microbots. That'd be cool. Hmm, maybe *I* should invent them!"

"*After* we've solved this case," Rora said.

Ziggy noticed a cafeteria worker moving dozens of boxes of bananas. The boxes were all around the kitchen. "Hey, Miss Lunch Lady! What's with all the bananas? I didn't see anything on the menu about banana pudding."

"No idea," said the lunch lady. "Someone left them here, but we didn't order them. It looks like we're going to have a banana menu tomorrow. We're making banana pudding, banana cake, and banana meatballs."

"This is the work of the Bandit!"
Rider said. "I bet he's craving
bananas and wants you to cook
up a bunch of treats
for him to steal!"

"I refuse to cook for that no-good thief!" said the lunch lady.

"Would you do it if your meal could help us catch the Lunchtime Bandit?" asked Rider. "I have a plan. It's *bananas*, but it just might work."

THE BANANA PLAN

Westie was covered in tape from head to tail. "If this doesn't get the Lunchtime Bandit's attention, then nothing will."

The pups had decorated the entire school with signs for the biggest banana split ever. Students were talking about it. Teachers were talking about it too.

Even the principal was talking about it—and nothing surprised the principal!

Rider, Rora, and Westie walked to the cafeteria.

"Okay, everyone, keep your eyes *peeled*," Rora said with a snicker. "Get it? Like banana peels."

Rider smiled. "Let's be serious. We need to catch this thief, and we can't afford to slip up. Now where's Ziggy?"

Just then a giant banana jumped at the pup detectives. It was Ziggy and he was so excited. "Guess what? They are giving out these banana costumes to every student to celebrate our big banana split," he explained. "Pretty cool, right?"

Sure enough, the hallways were filled with banana costumes. Banana fever had taken over the entire school.

Rider scratched his whiskers. "Actually it's not cool, Ziggy. The Lunchtime Bandit is onto us! Everyone looks the same."

The lunch bell rang and students in banana costumes flooded into the cafeteria. It was almost impossible to tell them apart. In the middle of the room was a giant banana split. All the students surrounded it and held their spoons in the air.

"One of these bananas must be the Bandit," Rora said. "Look for anything out of the ordinary."

"You mean like a room full of kids in banana costumes?" asked Westie.

"Over there!" cried Ziggy, pointing to the tallest banana costume in the crowd. "We know the Lunchtime Bandit is tall . . . tall like that banana!"

"Good call," said Rider. "Pup detectives, it's time to play fetch!"

The pups raced across the room, but the Bandit spotted them right away. He grabbed the banana split first and ran for the exit.

"Hey, that's *our* dessert!" the students shouted.

The four pups kept up the chase and were almost to the Bandit when the panda slipped out of his banana costume and threw it at them. Rider, Rora, Westie, and Ziggy became tangled in the giant banana peel. Luckily Ziggy was on the case. He ate the costume.

"Kid, that was not a real banana," said Rora.

"Yeah, but I was *real* hungry," said Ziggy.

Suddenly, a lunch lady walked in front of the pups carrying a tray of banana cream pies.

"I need to borrow these," Rora said. She grabbed the tray and hurled the pies at the Bandit.

Splat! Splat! Splat!

"Hey! You're not hitting him at all!" Ziggy cried. "Quit wasting yummy pies!"

Rora smiled. "Don't worry. I have excellent aim. I'm missing him on purpose and forcing the Bandit into the gym."

"The gym?" wondered Westie. "Well, I suppose he's going to need to work out after eating that entire banana split."

"Wrong, Westie," said Rider. "The front door is the only way in or out of the gym! Great thinking, Rora!"

The pups marched onto the basketball court. The Lunchtime Bandit was trapped!

"There's nowhere to go!" Rider shouted. "Get ready to do time for skipping the lunch line."

Rora added, "You found these

bananas too appealing. We knew
you would try to take the banana
split, so we turned it into
a banana *splat!*"

Westie pulled out a remote control. "Oh, you're going to go *bananas* over my new invention." He pressed the red button and the banana split burst into a flurry of chocolate fudge, whipped cream, and cherry sauce.

But the sauce explosion was bigger than Westie intended. The pup detectives were covered in ooey-gooey sweet stuff. By the time they shook off the sugary trap, the Bandit was gone.

One gym rope dangled down from the ceiling next to an open skylight.

"See?" Rora pointed upward. "I told you bad guys love skylights."

chapter
EIGHT

HOODWINKED

The grown-up Rider Woofson gave a long, heavy sigh. "That was our first case as a team."

The reporter was scribbling down notes frantically. "What about the Lunchtime Bandit?"

"We didn't get him," said Rider. "But that unsolved case brought us together as the P.I. Pack."

"Still . . . we'd love to solve that case," said Rora. She opened the old file and pulled out a piece of the gym rope with a chocolate and cherry paw print on it. "This is all

the evidence we have from that day. The Bandit climbed up the rope in the gym to escape, but he was sloppy. He left his paw print. One day we'll find him."

"That's quite a story," the reporter said as he held up his camera. "Why don't you put the evidence down and get together so I can take a group picture for the paper?"

"Sure," said Rider.

The other P.I. Pack members crowded together. Ziggy stepped on Westie's foot, Westie fell into Rora, and Rora's hair went up Rider's nose, making him sneeze. The reporter took a picture of the gang falling over one another.

The reporter laughed. "Hmm, maybe we should try that again."

Once the pack was settled, Scoops took another photo. This time he used a very bright flash that blinded the detectives.

As they rubbed their eyes,
Scoops yelped, "Thanks a lot!
Gotta *SPLIT*!"

"Well, that was rude," said
Ziggy with his eyes closed tight.
"His flash was way too powerful
for such a sunny day."

When Rider opened his eyes, he didn't like what he saw. The P.I. Pack's very first case file was not where he'd left it. In fact, it was gone!

Suddenly, there was a knock at the office door. Rider opened it and a ferret held out her paw. "Rider Woofson? I'm Farrah Ferret from the *Pawston Paw Print*. I'm here to interview you."

"Wait a minute!" Ziggy was confused. "We just had our interview."

Rora shook her head. "No, we didn't. That kangaroo wasn't a reporter. I'll bet anything that he was the Lunchtime Bandit, and he's just struck again!"

chapter
NINE

CASE CHASE

The detectives searched through the office. "Our very first case file is definitely missing," Rora said. "That fake reporter stole it! He got it all . . . the rope, the case file, everything!"

Rider faced the real reporter. "Miss Ferret, if you want a story, then follow us!"

The detectives ran outside, with Farrah Ferret following close behind.

Ziggy found their first clue right away. It was a kangaroo costume thrown into the bushes.

"Our fake reporter was a fake kangaroo, too? That makes me *hopping* mad!"

Just then Westie spotted some-one at the end of the block. The animal was holding a case file as he jumped into a getaway car. "Look, the Bandit is totally getting away . . . again!"

Quickly, the P.I. Pack, along with Farrah Ferret, climbed into their van. Rora revved the engine, hit the gas, and sped after the bad guy.

As they pulled closer, Rora noticed another clue. "P.I. Pack! Look at the getaway driver. It's Rotten Ruffhouse!"

"Well, that's just rotten luck," said Rider.

Meanwhile, in the Bandit's getaway car, Rotten Ruffhouse looked

in his rearview mirror. "Those detectives will never catch us."

"Well, make sure they don't," said the Bandit in the seat behind him. The bunny was busy reading through the case file.

"Did you get what you wanted?" asked Rotten.

"Oh yes," the bunny said with a sneer. "Those P.I. fools thought I was a reporter, and they spilled the beans of their very first case: the unsolved mystery of the Pawston Elementary Lunchtime Bandit!"

The words "spilled the beans" echoed inside Rotten's head as he drove. He thought back to the one horrible moment in elementary school that changed young Ronald Ruffhouse's life forever. "Wait. YOU were the Lunchtime Bandit?"

"I was, and I was never caught! I had so many disguises and stole so many lunches from under their noses, and they never sniffed me out," the bunny snarled.

"But . . . why?" Rotten asked.

"Because those selfish lunch ladies never gave me enough to eat, and I wanted more!" the bunny screamed. "I became the Lunchtime Bandit. That way, I could feast on whatever I wanted: kibble burgers, tuna tacos, even grass-flavored ice cream. Sure, it made me sick to my stomach,

105

but the crime kept me full! I stole everyone's food so they could feel as hungry as I once did!"

Rotten began to growl. He remembered what it felt like to be covered in rotten beans. Ever since that day, he could still hear all the other students chanting his awful, new name: "ROTTEN RUFFHOUSE! ROTTEN RUFFHOUSE!" Rotten suddenly turned the steering wheel to

the left. The whole car swerved around.

"Hey!" screamed the bunny. "This isn't the way to my hideout! What are you doing?"

Rotten gave the bunny a cool smile. "I'm about to spill the beans."

chapter
TEN

THE FIRST AND FINAL CASE

"What is going on?" the bunny asked. "Mr. Meow said that you were the best getaway driver he knows. That's why I hired you. Don't you know how to drive a getaway car? You use it to *get away*, *not* drive right back toward the scene of the crime!"

Rotten let out a rotten laugh.

"Don't worry. We're going to a new crime scene. I promise, you'll like it. But I hope you're hungry."

Now the bunny stared at the rottweiler in the front seat. "Hey, wait a minute. You look familiar. Have we met before?"

Rotten gave him a growling smile. "You could say we've *bean* around the block a few times."

The getaway car rocketed right past the P.I. Pack.

Ziggy yelped. "What's Rotten up to now?"

"There's only one way to find out," Rora said. She slammed on the brakes and made a sharp turn to spin the van around. Then she peeled out and chased after the bad guys.

"Where are they going?" asked Westie.

"They are going to jail!" Rider answered.

Westie pulled out a map of Pawston. "Hmm, are you sure? Because it looks like they are driving to the burrito factory."

Ziggy stuck his head out the window and took a big sniff. *"Bow-wowza!* That's not just a burrito factory. That's the old, deserted *bean* burrito factory! And from the smell of things, those beans have gone *rotten!"*

In the other car, the Lunchtime Bandit was freaking out. "Slow down, you fool! We're going to crash!"

But Rotten didn't slow down. He sped up. The car burst through the factory gates. The awful stench of stinky beans surrounded them.

The Lunchtime Bandit held his breath. "Stop!" he gasped. "Rotten! It smells so rotten!"

"That's my name—don't wear it out!" Rotten cheered as he pulled out a grappling hook. The evil dog launched it out the window and escaped from the car.

"Oh no!" yelled the Lunchtime Bandit as the car smashed right through the wall of the burrito factory. An avalanche of old, rotting, smelly beans washed all over the bad bunny.

The Lunchtime Bandit swam to the top of bean pile. "Gross! Rotten bean juice! It's awful! It's stinky! And it's in my ears! It's in my nose!"

Rotten stood safely on the roof of the building. He rubbed his paws together and looked down at the crusty criminal. Then he started to chant, "SMELLY BUNNY! SMELLY BUNNY!"

The P.I. Pack pulled up in their van, and Westie grabbed one of his first inventions—the Super

Soaker-Upper. "I knew I'd need this again!"

The invention soaked up the rotten bean sludge that oozed everywhere.

Rider pinched his nose and held up a pair of handcuffs. "All right, Scoops Hopper, or should I call you the Lunchtime Bandit? You are under arrest for crimes against school lunches."

The smelly bunny was green in the face. "Okay, you got me. Now please take me to jail. I need a bath!"

Then Farrah Ferret snapped a picture for her article. "I'll say. I'm going to call this the Case of the Not-Funny-Smelly-Bunny."

"I like the sound of that," said Rider, "but not the smell."